The
COLLINS BOOK OF
NURSERY TALES

Christmas 1996

To Hannah

wishing you a very happy
Christmas

with all our love,

Ruth, Brian, Victoria,
Matthew, Jonathan,
Nicholas & Benjamin

x x x x x x x

The Collins Book of Nursery Tales was first published by
HarperCollins Publishers Ltd in 1993
10 9 8 7 6 5 4 3 2 1
This compilation copyright © HarperCollins Publishers Ltd 1993

The Three Bears and Goldilocks and *The Story of Rumpelstiltskin* were
first published in single volumes by HarperCollins Publishers in 1991
Text & illustrations copyright © Jonathan Langley 1991
Little Red Riding Hood and *The Three Billy Goats Gruff* were first
published in single volumes by HarperCollins Publishers in 1992
Text & illustrations copyright © Jonathan Langley 1992
The Princess and the Frog and *The Ugly Duckling* were first
published in single volumes by HarperCollins Publishers in 1993
Text and illustrations copyright © Jonathan Langley 1993

A CIP catalogue record for this title is available
from the British Library.

ISBN: 0 00 193920-3

Printed and bound in Spain by Mateu Cromo

The
COLLINS BOOK OF
NURSERY TALES

RETOLD & ILLUSTRATED BY
JONATHAN LANGLEY

Collins
An Imprint of HarperCollinsPublishers

For Toby, Holly and Rosita

CONTENTS

LITTLE RED
RIDING HOOD

Once upon a time, on the edge of the big wood, there lived a little girl called Little Red Riding Hood. Her real name was Brenda but she was always known as Little Red Riding Hood because this was what her mother called her when she was a baby. Brenda used to wear a red bonnet when she went out for a ride in her pram, and she still wears it now.

One day Little Red Riding Hood was playing out in the sunshine when her mother called her, "I want you to go over to Grandma's house with some groceries. Grandma's not very well and she hasn't been able to get out to the shops."

"Do I have to?" said Little Red Riding Hood with a glum face.

"Yes you do!" said Mum. "Now go and wash your face." Mum packed the groceries into a basket while Little Red Riding Hood did as she was told.

When the basket was ready Mum looked at Little Red Riding Hood very seriously,

"Now, I want you to be very sensible," she said. "Go straight through the wood to Grandma's house. Don't mess about. Stay on the path and don't talk to any strangers."

She kissed Little Red Riding Hood on top of her head, handed her the basket of groceries, and pushed her out of the door. Little Red Riding Hood scowled and stomped off down the path into the wood.

Little Red Riding Hood hadn't been walking far when she heard a rustling in the trees. Then she heard a deep, silky voice calling, "Little girl, little girl, can you spare a minute?"

Little Red Riding Hood was curious and strayed off the path to see where the voice was coming from. It seemed to come from the dark shadows behind the trees. There was a funny smell of old dogs and, for a moment, she thought she saw a tall woolly figure. She remembered what her mum had said but the voice was quite friendly.

"What do you want?" said Little Red Riding Hood boldly.

"Where are you going little girl?" said the voice.

"I'm going to Grandma's house. She's not well and I'm taking her some groceries," said Little Red Riding Hood.

"How kind," said the voice. "What a good girl you must be. And where does your poor grandmother live?"

Little Red Riding Hood smiled angelically and replied in her sweetest voice, "She lives at the far side of the wood, next to the pond."

"What a pleasant place to live," said the soft voice, "but you mustn't keep the old lady waiting. Off you go, dear."

Little Red Riding Hood waved and continued on to Grandma's house.

When Little Red Riding Hood was out of sight the tall woolly figure stepped out of the shadows and smiled a big sharp-toothed smile.

The silky voice belonged to a wolf!

He was hungry and wanted to eat Little Red Riding Hood but he was also clever. He was too near the little girl's house and her mother might hear her scream.

If he took the short cut through the trees, he thought, he
could arrive at Grandma's house before Little Red Riding
Hood, and then he could eat the tasty little girl and her fat
old grandmother. Licking his lips he raced off into the
dark wood.

When the wolf reached Grandma's house he sneaked around the back and peeked in through the kitchen window. Grandma was making a pot of tea. The wolf lifted the latch silently and tip-toed in when Grandma's back was turned. Then, before Grandma could shout, 'tea-bag!' the greedy wolf swallowed her whole.

"Mmm, yum, yum," he said. Then, he hurried to Grandma's bedroom and searched her drawers until he found a big pink nightgown and a frilly nightcap.

Quickly the wolf dressed himself in Grandma's clothes and leapt into bed just as he heard Little Red Riding Hood approaching the house.

"Grandma, where are you?" shouted Little Red Riding Hood.

"I'm in bed, child," called the wolf in his best 'old lady' voice. "Come right in, the door's not locked."

Little Red Riding Hood opened the back door and stepped into the kitchen. There was a funny smell which was different from Grandma's smell, and the teapot lay broken on the floor.

"Grandma, are you all right?" called Little Red Riding Hood.

"Yes dear, I'm not feeling myself today so I decided to go back to bed. Do come in and see me."

It was dark in Grandma's room because the curtains were drawn. Little Red Riding Hood, still holding the basket of groceries, stood beside the bed. How strange, she thought, there was that funny smell of old dogs again. She looked at the figure under the great heap of bedclothes and frowned.

"Grandma, are you sure you're all right?" said Little Red Riding Hood.

"Of course, my child. I'm just a bit under the weather," said the wolf.

Little Red Riding Hood thought Grandma's voice sounded strange, but she did have a bad cold. Then she noticed Grandma's ears.

"Grandma, what big ears you have!"

"All the better to hear you with, my dear," said the wolf.

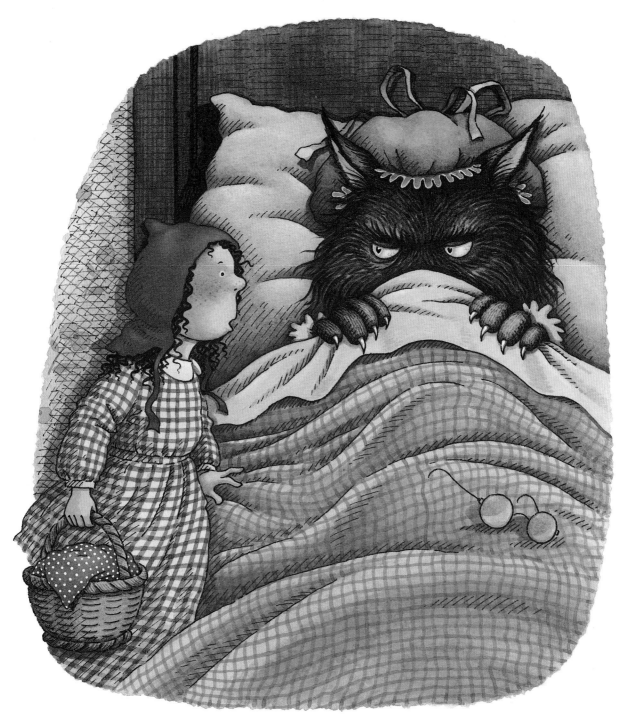

Then Little Red Riding Hood noticed Grandma's gleaming eyes.

"Grandma, what big eyes you have!"

"All the better to see you with, my dear," said the wolf.

Then, as Little Red Riding Hood's eyes became accustomed to the dim light, she noticed Grandma's pointed nose and shining teeth.

"Grandma, what big teeth you have!"

At this the wolf leapt up and growled, "ALL THE BETTER TO EAT YOU WITH, MY DEAR!"

The wolf's jaws were all around her but, quick as a flash, Little Red Riding Hood swung the shopping basket and hit the wolf squarely on the nose. He yelped and fell back.

At that moment the door burst open and there stood Mum with Grandma's frying pan in her hand! She lifted it high above her head, then brought it down with a CLANG! on the wicked wolf's head.

He did not move again.

Little Red Riding Hood ran to her mother who hugged her tight. "Mum, why are you here?" she said.

"I had a funny feeling in my bones," said Mum, "so I decided to come and see how Grandma was for myself. Where is she?"

There was a muffled cry from where the wolf was lying and something was moving in the wolf's tummy!

"Quick, Little Red Riding Hood, get the scissors," said Mum. With a snip, snip, snip, Mum cut open the wolf's tummy and out spilled an angry Grandma. She was shaken but, luckily, not harmed in any way.

"I'm going to teach that wolf a lesson," said Grandma.
"Fetch me my sewing basket Little Red Riding Hood."
  Grandma worked quickly. From under the kitchen sink she pulled a sack of onions. She stuffed them all into the wolf's tummy then, with her best embroidery stitches, sewed up the woolly beast's belly.

Then Grandma, Mum and Little Red Riding Hood together rolled the sleeping wolf across the floor and out of the door. Grandma slammed the door shut.

"Put the kettle on Little Red Riding Hood, what we need now is a cup of tea," said Grandma, who was feeling much better.

When the wolf woke up he felt terrible. His head hurt and his tummy felt as though it was on fire. "Ooooh," he said to himself, "I'll never eat another grandma again."

He never did, and he never talked to strange girls again either.

THE THREE BEARS
AND GOLDILOCKS

Once upon a time, there were three bears who lived in a
little house in the big wood. There was a great big bear
called George, a middle-sized bear called Mavis and a tiny
little bear called Brian; but they were better known
as Father Bear, Mother Bear and Baby Bear, or The
Three Bears.

The Three Bears lived very happily and quietly together in their house which was always tidy. They each had their own things. They had their own food bowls: a big one with daisies on for Father Bear, a middle-sized one with buttercups on for Mother Bear and a little one with rabbits on for Baby Bear.

They had their own chairs: a big one with a high back and arms for Father Bear, a middle-sized one with big cushions for Mother Bear and a little one with rabbits on for Baby Bear. They had their own beds: a big one with a carved headboard for Father Bear, a middle-sized one with a quilted headboard for Mother Bear and a little one with rabbits on for Baby Bear.

One morning, when it was his turn to make breakfast,
Father Bear made a big pot of porridge. When it was
ready, he poured it into the three bowls. It was still too
hot to eat so Father Bear suggested, as it was a sunny
morning, that they all go for a stroll in the woods while
the porridge cooled. After opening all the windows to let
the sun in to warm the house, they set off down the path.

On that same morning there was someone else walking in the big wood. A little girl called Goldilocks was stomping along swatting at butterflies with a stick and kicking the heads off flowers. She was in a bad mood. Her mum had told her off and she'd slammed out of the house without any breakfast.

Goldilocks was feeling very hungry when she suddenly smelled the warm, delicious smell of porridge. She followed the smell with her nose until she came to where The Three Bears' house stood in a sunny clearing.

Goldilocks liked the look
of the house and, when
she peeped through the open
window, she saw three bowls
of porridge on the table.
Goldilocks' empty tummy
grumbled. She wondered
if whoever lived in
the house might like to
share their breakfast
with her, so she
knocked on the door.
There was no reply.
Goldilocks then lifted
the latch to see if the
door was locked. It
wasn't. After looking
around, she opened
the door, stepped
inside, and went
straight for the
bowls of porridge
on the table.

She first tried the biggest
bowl with the most amount
of porridge in it.

"Oooh!" said Goldilocks.
"Too hot."

Then she tried the
middle-sized bowl.

"Yuk, too cold!" she said.

Next she tried the little
bowl with the rabbits on.

"Yum, yum just right," she
said, and quickly ate it all up.

Goldilocks then started to make herself at home.

She tried sitting in the biggest chair but it was
very uncomfortable.

"Too hard," said Goldilocks.

Aaarrggh!

Then she tried the
middle-sized chair.

"Too soft," she said.

Next she tried the little chair.

"Mmm, just right," she said.
She liked this one and wriggled
with glee, so much so that –
CRASH! – the back legs broke
and she fell to the floor.

Picking herself up, and feeling a bit cross, Goldilocks then decided to explore the rest of the house. She went upstairs to the bedroom where she found the three beds.

First she tried lying on the biggest bed.

"Too high," she said.

Then she tried lying on the middle-sized bed.

"Too low," said Goldilocks.

Next she tried the little bed.
  "Aaah, just right," she said.
It was so comfortable that she immediately
fell fast asleep.

Very soon The Three Bears returned home from their walk and were surprised to find the door open. They looked inside and noticed the bowls of porridge on the table.

"Somebody has been eating my porridge!" said Father Bear in a great, gruff, growling voice.

"Somebody has been eating my porridge!" said Mother Bear in a mellow, middle-sized voice.

"Somebody has been eating my porridge, and has eaten it all up!" cried Baby Bear in a squeaky, little voice.

Then they noticed the chairs had been moved.

"Somebody has been sitting in my chair!"
said Father Bear in a great, gruff, growling voice.

"Somebody has been sitting in my chair!" said Mother Bear in a mellow, middle-sized voice.

"Somebody has been sitting in my chair, and broken it all to bits!" sobbed Baby Bear in a squeaky, little voice, dripping tears on to the floor.

The Three Bears then heard the sound of snoring coming from upstairs.

They tiptoed up the stairs and into the bedroom. They
looked at the rumpled beds.

"Somebody has been lying on my bed!"
said Father Bear in a great, gruff, growling voice.

"Somebody has been lying on my bed!" said
Mother Bear in a mellow, middle-sized voice.

"Somebody has been lying on my bed, and she's still there!"
wailed Baby Bear in a squeaky, little voice.

This commotion woke Goldilocks up with a start. Seeing
The Three Bears she screamed.
"EEEEAAAWWAAAGHH!"

This so frightened The Three Bears that they all flung up their arms and they screamed too.

"EEEEEEAAAAWWWAAAAGGHH!"

Goldilocks thought she was going to be eaten! She leaped out of bed and dived out of the nearest window. She landed in a blackberry bush, picked herself up, and ran off home as fast as her legs would go.

After The Three Bears got over their shock, Father Bear made some more porridge, Mother Bear mended Baby Bear's chair and Baby Bear made the beds.

They lived happily ever after and always locked their door when they went out, just in case.

Goldilocks never went back to The Three Bears' house. She grew up into a fine young woman and had many adventures, but she never did eat porridge again.

THE STORY OF
RUMPELSTILTSKIN

Once upon a time, long, long ago, when mountains were
more pointed and there was a king in every castle, there
lived a miller who was forever telling tall stories. The
miller had a daughter called Ruby, who was very clever, and
he was always boasting about the things she could do.

Once he boasted that his daughter sang so beautifully that
the birds came out at night and flew around the moon.
Another time he said his daughter could juggle four
hedgehogs with one hand and make a dozen fruit cakes
with the other.

These stories were so silly that his neighbours just laughed when they heard them, but one day the King was in town and he heard one of the miller's stories.

"My daughter is so clever that she can spin straw into gold," the miller said.

The King loved gold and, when he heard the miller's
boast, he ordered Ruby to be brought to his castle and
led her to a small room where there was a spinning
wheel and straw piled up to the ceiling.

"Spin this straw into gold by morning or you will be fed to the Royal Crocodiles," the King said, and locked her in.

Poor Ruby was both cross and frightened. "What has my stupid father done now. I can't spin straw into gold," she said. She looked at the straw and thought about the Royal Crocodiles and began to cry.

Suddenly a funny little man appeared and skipped around the room. "Well now, what's all this? Why are you crying?" he said.

"I must spin this straw into gold and I don't know how," answered Ruby.

The little man smiled and said, "What will you give me if I spin the straw into gold for you?"

"I will give you my necklace," said Ruby.

"Very well," said the little man and held out his hand.
Ruby gave him the necklace and he put it in his pocket.
Then he sat down at the spinning wheel and started to
spin. He really was spinning straw into gold!

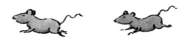

All through the night the little man worked at the spinning wheel and, by morning, all the straw was gone and in its place was a heap of glistening gold thread. Ruby stared at the gold in amazement.

"Oh thank you," she said to the little man, but he'd disappeared.

When the King came and unlocked the door he gasped at
the sight of all the gold. He thought Ruby was indeed
very clever, but he was a very greedy King. That night he
took Ruby to a bigger room with a spinning wheel and
straw piled up to the ceiling.

"Spin this straw into gold by morning or you will be fed to the Royal Crocodiles," the King said, and again he locked her in.

Ruby sat at the spinning wheel and tried to spin the straw but all she made was dust. "Oh, if only that little man could help me," she cried.

"Here I am," said a voice, and there he was again. "What will you give me if I spin all this straw into gold for you?" said the funny little man.

"I will give you my ring," said Ruby, and quickly put it in his hand.

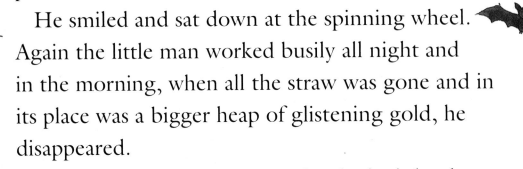

He smiled and sat down at the spinning wheel. Again the little man worked busily all night and in the morning, when all the straw was gone and in its place was a bigger heap of glistening gold, he disappeared.

At sunrise the King came and unlocked the door. He was delighted to see all the gold. "You are indeed very, very clever," he said, but he was a very, very greedy king and he wanted even more.

That night he took Ruby to an even bigger room with a spinning wheel and straw piled up to the ceiling.

"Spin this straw into gold by morning or you will be fed to the Royal Crocodiles," the King said, and once again he locked her in.

Ruby looked at the mountain of straw and said, "Oh, what am I to do? Only that little man can help me now."

"Here I am," said a voice, and once again there he was. "What will you give me if I spin all this straw into gold for you?" said the funny little man.

"I have nothing more to give you," said Ruby.

"Then promise to give me your first baby when you are Queen," said the little man.

Ruby thought this could never happen, so she promised.

Once again the little man worked all night at the spinning wheel until all the straw was gone and in its place was a huge heap of glistening gold. Then, as before, he disappeared.

Once more the King came and unlocked the door. He was overjoyed to see all the gold. "You are the cleverest in all my kingdom," he said. "Marry me and we will be rich for ever."

Ruby was a bit shocked but, since there was no more talk of crocodiles, she said, "Yes."

Soon there was a grand Royal Wedding and Ruby and the King were married. They were very happy together and, when their first baby was born, they were even happier, but Queen Ruby forgot her promise to the little man.

73

One day he came when Queen Ruby was alone and reminded her. She cried and cried until, at last, the little man said, "If you can guess my name in three days you can keep your child." Then he disappeared.

All day and night Ruby sat thinking of all the names she knew, and she sent messengers all over the kingdom to find new ones.

Next day, when the little man came, Queen Ruby said, "Is it Thomas, Kevin, or Michael?"

"No, no, no," said the little man, and skipped away.

The next day Queen Ruby tried more unusual names. "Is it Bandylegs, Jellybottom, or Crookshanks?"

"No, no, no," said the little man skipping away. "If you can't guess my name tomorrow, I will take the baby."

On the morning of the third day Queen Ruby was feeling very unhappy when a messenger returned and said, "Yesterday I was in the great dark wood, when I came upon a funny little house. In front of the house was a fire, and a strange little man was dancing around the fire singing:

'Hocus pocus, dance and sing
First a necklace, then a ring
Riddles and magic are my game
RUMPELSTILTSKIN is my name!'"

Queen Ruby jumped for joy. "Thank you, thank you!" she said to the messenger and gave her a bag of gold.

When the funny little man appeared, Queen Ruby pretended not to know and said, "Is your name Jack, or is it Percy, or is it …

R U M P E L S T I L T S K I N ? "

"Aaaaahh!! Someone told you!" shouted the little man.
He jumped about, all in a rage, and stamped his foot so
hard it went through the floor where it stuck fast. Red in
the face, he pulled and pulled at his leg, then, with a cry
of anger, he disappeared in a puff of smoke.

Ruby lived happily ever after. She was a good Queen and well loved by the people and, after the birth of her second child, it was decreed that she and her children should rule the country, leaving the King to count his treasure.

The King had a long life but one day, whilst he was carrying a heavy sack of gold, he accidentally fell into the Royal Crocodile Pool and was never seen again.

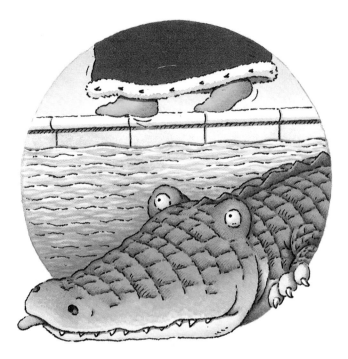

THE THREE BILLY GOATS GRUFF

Once upon a time, in a land beyond the high mountains and over the sea, there were three billy goats who lived on a rocky hillside. There was a big billy goat, a middle-sized billy goat, and a little billy goat, and they were all called Gruff.

The three Billy Goats Gruff had always lived on the
hillside and every day they did nothing but eat from
morning till night. The other goats who lived there
were happy to eat the rough grass that grew between the
stones, the moss that grew on the rocks, and the leaves
and twigs that grew on the trees; but the three Billy Goats
Gruff wanted more.

They dreamed of going down into the valley, trotting across the bridge which joined the rocky hillside to the lush green meadow on the other side of the river and eating until they were fat.

But the bridge was the only way across the river, which was deep and fast flowing, and under the bridge lived a Troll. He was as frightening to look at as he was fierce and would gobble up anyone who tried to cross to the other side and no one dared to try.

One day, when the three Billy Goats Gruff were again moaning about the coarse grass and dry leaves, an old grandfather billy goat, who was eating nearby, laughed and said,

"Perhaps you should all go and feast yourselves in the big meadow."

"Perhaps we should!" replied the little Billy Goat Gruff, cheekily.

"And what about the river?" said the grandfather billy goat. "And the Troll?"

"I'm not afraid of the Troll," said the big Billy Goat Gruff.

"Neither am I," said the middle-sized Billy Goat Gruff.

"Nor me," said the little Billy Goat Gruff. "We'll go right now!"

The other two Billy Goats Gruff looked at the little Billy Goat Gruff, then at each other. They hadn't intended this to happen and were rather shocked.

"Well, are all you brave Billy Goats Gruff going?" taunted the grandfather billy goat.

"Er... yes, of course we are," said the big Billy Goat Gruff. "We're not frightened."

Really they were all very frightened, but now they had to go, or look foolish.

"Goodbye, Billy Goats Gruff. I don't expect we'll see you again," said the old grandfather billy goat.

The three Billy Goats Gruff started off down the hillside, slowly at first, then faster and faster as it became a race to the bottom.

When they reached the river they looked at the deep rushing water. If only they could swim across, they all thought. They gazed over at the green meadow. It made them feel hungry, but also afraid.

They looked again across the river. The sun was shining on the lush green grass and clover and speckles of sweet flowers sparkled in the sunlight.

Determinedly they made their way along the river bank to the big wooden bridge.

Standing well back, they tried to look underneath at
what might be lurking in the shadows, but it was too dark
and gloomy to see.

(Deep within the darkness lay the Troll asleep. He'd
been fishing all night but had caught nothing, which had
made him very grumpy.)

"Perhaps the Troll has gone away?" said the little Billy Goat Gruff hopefully.

"Perhaps he has," said the middle-sized Billy Goat Gruff. "Since this was your idea, you go first and see. We'll just wait here."

The middle-sized Billy Goat Gruff and the big Billy Goat Gruff stepped back, leaving the little Billy Goat Gruff standing alone.

The little Billy Goat Gruff was afraid. He turned to look at his brothers, then, with his head held high, bravely set off across the bridge.

TRIP, TRAP! TRIP, TRAP! TRIP, TRAP! TRIP, TRAP! went his hooves on the wooden boards. He was nearly in the middle and thought he was going to get safely across when suddenly the monstrous Troll popped his head out from beneath the bridge.

"Who's that trip-trapping over my bridge?" roared the Troll, rubbing his eyes.

"It's only me," said the little Billy Goat Gruff in his little voice, "I'm going across to the meadow to make myself fat."

"Oh no you're not!" roared the Troll. "You've woken me up and now I'm coming to gobble you up!"

"No, no, don't eat me," bleated the little Billy Goat Gruff. "I'm the littlest Billy Goat Gruff. I'm too small and bony. Wait until the second Billy Goat Gruff comes along. He's much bigger and fatter."

"Very well," said the Troll angrily, "be off with you!"

So the little Billy Goat Gruff crossed the bridge and skipped off into the meadow to eat the sweet grass.

When the middle-sized Billy Goat Gruff saw that his
brother had reached the meadow safely, he felt much
braver and he too set off across the bridge.

TRIP, TRAP! TRIP, TRAP! TRIP, TRAP! TRIP,
TRAP! went his hooves on the wooden boards. He was
nearly in the middle when again out popped the Troll's
head, looking very fierce, from beneath the bridge.

"Who's that trip-trapping over my bridge?" roared the Troll.

"It's only me," said the middle-sized Billy Goat Gruff in his middle-sized voice. "I'm going across to the meadow to make myself fat."

"Oh no you're not!" roared the Troll. "I'm coming to gobble you up!"

"No, no, don't eat me," pleaded the middle-sized Billy Goat Gruff. "I'm not a very big Billy Goat Gruff. There's a much bigger one than me. Wait until the third Billy Goat Gruff comes along. He's much bigger and fatter."

"Very well," said the Troll even angrier, "be off with you!"

So the middle-sized Billy Goat Gruff crossed the bridge and skipped off into the meadow to join his brother eating the sweet grass.

Then there was only the big Billy Goat Gruff left to cross. He puffed himself up to make him feel very strong and brave, then he too set off across the bridge.

TRIP, TRAP! TRIP, TRAP! TRIP, TRAP! TRIP, TRAP! stamped his hooves on the wooden boards. He was nearly in the middle when, once again, out popped the Troll's head looking fiercer than ever.

"Who's that trip-trapping over my
bridge?" roared the Troll.
   "It's me, the biggest Billy Goat Gruff,"
bellowed the big Billy Goat Gruff in his great big voice,
"and I'm going across to the meadow to
make myself fat!"

"Oh no you're not!" roared the Troll, even louder than before, **"I'm coming to gobble you up!"**

The Troll leapt up onto the bridge and started gnashing his teeth but the big Billy Goat Gruff stamped his hooves, then lowered his horns, and charged!

Thundering over the wooden boards, with steam coming out of his nostrils, he tossed the Troll high in the air. Up, up he went, so high he circled the moon, then down, down he fell – SPLASH! – into the middle of the deep river and was never seen again.

The Big Billy Goat Gruff crossed the bridge and skipped off into the meadow to join his brothers.

Then the three Billy Goats Gruff ate the sweet grass until they were fat, and then they ate until their tummies hurt, and then they ate until they couldn't move, and then they went to sleep for a long, long time.

The three Billy Goats Gruff had a long and happy life. They all grew up to be old grandfather Billy Goats Gruff with great curling horns and long grey beards.

Sometimes they went back over the bridge to see their friends on the rocky hillside, but whenever they did, they galloped across as fast as they could just in case the Troll had come back.

THE PRINCESS
AND THE FROG

Once upon a time, long ago, when the world was not as it always has been and rivers flowed uphill as well as down, there lived a king who had seven daughters. The six elder daughters had each gone to seek their way in the world, only Ivy, the youngest daughter, still lived at home.

Ivy was not like her older sisters, who were very fine and sensible and enjoyed doing royal things such as wearing crowns and going to grand balls. Ivy was happiest playing in the fields and woods that surrounded her father's castle. She especially liked to play with the beautiful, shiny, golden ball which her father had given her. It was the most treasured of all her possessions.

One bright sunny morning Ivy gulped down her breakfast, then ran out of the castle and into the fields, kicking her golden ball ahead of her. She ran across one field, then another, until she reached the edge of the big wood where she kicked the ball as hard as she could. Ivy watched as it rose high in the air, over the top of some smaller trees, then down through the branches of a tall oak until it fell - SPLASH! - into the middle of a deep pool where it sank out of sight.

Quickly Ivy found a long stick and prodded around in the pool, but she couldn't feel the ball anywhere and all she fished out was mud and weed.

Ivy was feeling desperate and began to cry.

"BOO HOO HOO!" she wailed and sobbed.

Then she heard a voice saying, "Princess, why are you crying?" Ivy looked around to see where the voice was coming from. All she could see was a green frog sitting on a rock by the pool.

"Did you say something?" said Ivy.

"Yes," said the frog. "What has made you so upset?"

"My beautiful golden ball has fallen into the pool and I can't get it out," said Ivy. "The water is so deep and I can't swim... BOO HOO HOO!"

"Don't cry," said the frog. "I can find your ball. But what will you give me if I do?"

"I will give you anything you want," said Ivy. "You can have my jewels, my fancy royal clothes, even my best crown, if only you will find my golden ball."

"I do not want your jewels or your clothes or even your golden crown. I want to be your friend. I want to sit beside you at the table, eat from your golden plate and drink from your golden cup. I want to sleep on a silk cushion beside your pretty bed. And I want you to kiss me goodnight before you sleep. If you promise me these things," said the frog, "I will find your golden ball."

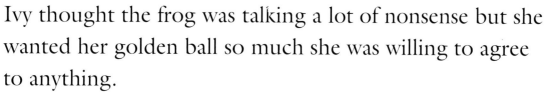

Ivy thought the frog was talking a lot of nonsense but she
wanted her golden ball so much she was willing to agree
to anything.

"I promise all you ask," she said, "if only you will find
my golden ball."

The frog smiled and said, "Remember, you've
promised." Then he dived down deep into the pool.

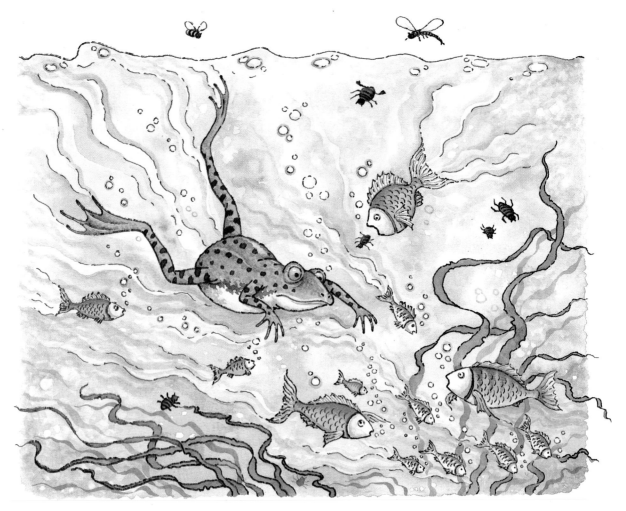

After a long time the frog came swimming up again with the golden ball. Ivy was overjoyed!

The frog threw the ball on to the grass beside Ivy and she picked it up and hugged it. Then she turned and ran off home as fast as she could.

Quickly the frog hopped out of the water.

"Wait for me! Wait for me!" he croaked.

He hopped along trying to catch up but was soon left far behind. Without looking back Ivy kept on running across the fields towards her father's castle.

A week and a day later Ivy had forgotten all about the frog. She was sitting at dinner with the King and all his courtiers when a messenger entered the great hall and announced, "Your Majesty, there is a frog at the door who says that Princess Ivy promised to share her dinner with him."

Ivy looked shocked and her face turned red.

"Is this true, Ivy?" said the King, looking very surprised.

"Well... it is a bit true," said Ivy. Then she told her father what had happened in the big wood and what the frog had asked of her. "I promised him that he could come and live with me," she said, "but I never thought he would follow me all the way home. I don't want to live with a slimy old frog."

The King was a good and honest man who never told a lie and always kept his word. He shook his head and said, "My dear, when a promise is made it must be kept. You must ask the frog to dine with you."

Ivy felt ashamed and reluctantly asked the messenger to show the frog in.

Presently the frog hopped into the great hall and sat by Ivy's chair.

"You promised I could sit beside you," said the frog. Ivy couldn't bear to touch the frog so she picked it up with her napkin and put it on the table. The frog smiled at her and sat beside her plate.

Ivy called for a servant to bring some beetles and pondweed for him but the frog said, "No, I want to eat what you eat, Princess. You promised I could eat from your golden plate and drink from your golden cup."

The thought of this made Ivy feel quite sick and she didn't want to eat any more. The frog, however, enjoyed every bite.

When he had finished the frog said to Ivy, "Now I'm tired, please take me to your room."

Ivy turned to the King and said, "Do I have to?" The King looked at her sternly and said, "Yes, you do. The frog helped you when you were in need and you made him a promise."

So Ivy carried the frog to her bedroom, but as she passed her maid she whispered, "Bring a fishtank with a lid to my bedroom, now."

When the maid brought the fishtank (in which she'd put a stone and some tadpoles to keep the frog company) Ivy quickly popped the frog inside and shut the lid, then she climbed into bed.

"No, no, no," said the frog, jumping up and down, "you promised I could sleep on a silk cushion beside your bed!" And he jumped up and down so much he knocked the lid off the fishtank and hopped out. "If you don't put me on a cushion beside your bed I shall tell the King you do not keep your promises."

Ivy remembered what her father had said. With tears in her eyes she picked up the frog and put him on a silk cushion beside her bed. How unhappy she was. She didn't want to live with a green frog for the rest of her life!

"Now kiss me goodnight," the frog said.

"Oh, how horrible!" thought Ivy, but again, she knew her father would insist. Trying to pretend she was somewhere else, she leaned over, closed her eyes, pursed her lips... and kissed the frog...

Suddenly the room was filled with bright lights and stars!
Ivy opened her eyes and couldn't believe what she saw.
The frog had disappeared! He had turned into a
handsome prince!

"Oh thank you, thank you!" he said. Then he told Ivy how a wicked witch had put a spell on him and turned him into a frog. The spell could only be broken if a beautiful princess would befriend him, eat with him, sleep beside him and kiss him.

The Frog Prince, whose name was Frederick, told Princess Ivy how he had seen her playing with her golden ball in the wood and had fallen in love with her.

Princess Ivy blushed. "We must tell my father what has happened," she said. The King was very surprised when he saw Prince Frederick with Ivy but he was so glad that she was not going to live with a frog.

Princess Ivy and Prince Freddy, as he was better known,
became the best of friends and were always together. On
sunny days they played in the fields with Princess Ivy's
golden ball, or in the wood where Prince Freddy taught
Princess Ivy how to swim; and on wet days they played
indoors with Prince Freddy's aquarium.

After a year and a day Princess Ivy and Prince Freddy were married. The King was delighted and there were celebrations throughout the land. Within seven years the Princess and Prince had seven children, who were surprisingly good at both swimming and leapfrog, and they all lived happily ever after.

THE UGLY DUCKLING

Once upon a time, on a dark and stormy night, a great
wild wind blew down from the hills. It whistled through
the woods and across the fields to the river where it blew
a poor mother duck right out of her nest.

"Oh dear," she said, picking herself up, "I must get
back to my eggs!"

She stumbled around in the dark until she found her
nest then, exhausted, she settled down again on the eggs
to keep them warm.

In the morning the storm had passed and the sun came up warm and bright. The mother duck awoke when she felt something move beneath her.

The eggs were rocking to and fro. She counted them, "One, two, three, four, five, six ... seven?" She had only laid six eggs but now there were seven, and one was much bigger than the rest.

"I don't remember that one," she said. "Seven eggs, I am a lucky duck!"

Soon, one by one, the smaller eggs broke open and out popped six pretty little yellow ducklings. But the biggest egg had not hatched.

 The six ducklings gathered around the big egg and
watched as the mother duck sat on top of it for a day and
a night until the egg, at last, began to stir. Slowly it cracked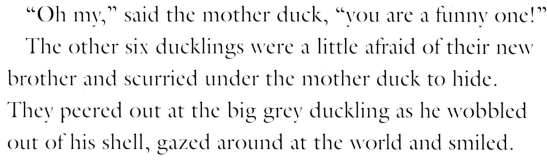
open and out tumbled a big scruffy duckling with grey
 feathers and very big black feet.

"Oh my," said the mother duck, "you are a funny one!"

The other six ducklings were a little afraid of their new
brother and scurried under the mother duck to hide.
They peered out at the big grey duckling as he wobbled
out of his shell, gazed around at the world and smiled.

"Oh well," said the mother duck, "he looks happy and
healthy," and cuddled him to her with the other ducklings.

Next day the mother duck led her new family down to the river for a swimming lesson. The six little yellow ducklings scampered down the bank after their mother while the big grey duckling followed clumsily behind. One by one they jumped in the water. The yellow ducklings struggled and splashed but the grey duckling found his big feet very useful and he swam straight away. The other ducklings tried to keep up with him but the big duckling was much too fast.

"Oh well," said the mother duck, "he may not be a beauty but he can certainly swim."

One day the mother duck took her ducklings to visit some
friends in the farmyard. The farm ducks were thrilled to
see the new yellow ducklings.

"What little beauties!" they said, fussing around and
patting them. Then they saw the big grey duckling.

"What is that?" said one old duck.

"What a strange awkward creature," said another.

The big grey duckling became shy and hid behind his
mother but she was proud of all her offspring and urged
him on saying, "And this is my big strong son."

The big duckling stuck out his chest and stepped forward but tripped over his feet and fell head first in a muddy puddle. The farm ducks all laughed, "Ha, ha, ha, what a mess!"

The mother duck tried to help him. "Leave him alone!" she said. "He may not be pretty but he's gentle and brave." But the other ducks rolled about laughing.

"Ha, ha, ha, what a clumsy cluck! What an ugly duckling!"

Other animals came over to see what the joke was. When the hens saw the big duckling they laughed too, and so did the pigs, and the sheep, and the cow, and the horse.

The duckling looked around at all the laughing animals and frowned.

"I don't belong here!" he said and ran out of the farmyard and away across the fields.

The duckling ran on and on until he came to the great marsh where the wild ducks live. He was tired and sat down to rest in a clump of reeds.

"I know I'm not little, yellow and fluffy like my brothers and sisters," he said to himself. "But I'm me! I may be scruffy and grey and I may have big black feet, but I'm as good as they are."

Three wild ducks were flying past and saw him sitting in the reeds.

"Look, there's a mumbling duckling with big feet!" said one and they all laughed.

The duckling looked up and stuck his tongue out at them, he didn't care. The wild ducks flew away laughing loudly. "See you again flipper feet," they called.

"I'll show them," said the duckling.

He fell asleep and dreamed he was with other ducklings just like himself, but suddenly – BANG! BANG! BANG! – the duckling awoke with a start. Men were shooting at ducks all around!

He put his wings over his head and tried to hide but then something came rushing towards him through the marsh – a huge dog with a big red tongue and sharp teeth!

The duckling jumped into a pool and hid under the water until the dog had gone.

"I don't belong here!" said the duckling. "This is a terrible place!" and he hurried away from the marsh.

 As darkness fell he came to the big wood. Strange noises and shadows seemed to follow him as he waddled along the path through the tall trees.

"I don't belong here," he whispered.

Soon he came to a tumbledown cottage where a light shone from a window. The house belonged to an old woman who lived with her cat and a hen. The duckling was cold and tired and he could see it was warm inside, so he crept in through a crack in the door.

The old woman was pleased to see him. "Now I shall have eggs from a duck as well as a hen," she said, and made a place for the duckling by the fire.

When the old woman went to bed the cat and the hen cornered the duckling.

"Can you lay eggs?" said the hen.

"No," said the duckling, "but I can swim."

"Can you purr?" said the cat.

"No," replied the duckling, "but I can dive."

"Swim and dive indeed! You're no use to our mistress," they both said.

"I don't care!" said the duckling and waddled out of the door and into the night. "I don't belong here," he said.

The duckling journeyed on and on over hills and dales looking for a place to call home. Eventually he found a small lake where he lived on his own and no one bothered him.

Many weeks passed and the leaves on the trees turned from green to brown. The days were shorter and the duckling shivered through the long nights.

One evening, as the sun was setting, he heard a strange sound in the sky and looked up to see a flock of the most beautiful birds. They were magical white birds with great outstretched wings and long graceful necks.

One of them gave a strange cry that he seemed to understand and he wished he could go with them.

Soon the cold winds of winter blew and the lake, where the duckling lived, began to freeze. He swam round and round to keep warm but the water froze around his feet and he was stuck fast.

Next morning a kind farmer passed by and saw the duckling. He smashed the ice and carried the frozen bird home and put him by the fire to warm up. The duckling felt happy and safe but when the farmer's children came home they were noisy and frightened him.

He flapped his wings to try to get away from them and knocked over a bowl of milk. Their mother tried to catch him but he flew into the butter tub and then fell in the flour barrel. Milk, butter and flour were spilled all over the floor! The farmer shouted, the mother shouted, the children shouted too!

"I don't belong here!" said the duckling, and ran out of the door.

On and on he ran through the snow until he could run no more and there he curled up in a hollow and slept for the rest of the long cold winter.

He awoke beside a large lake with the sun on his back and the larks singing overhead. Spring had come at last. The grass was green, there was blossom on the trees, and he was feeling much stronger.

He wandered down to the water and swam away from the bank. He was enjoying himself when, from behind some tall rushes, sailed three of the beautiful white birds he had seen flying so high, and they were coming towards him. He thought they were going to call him names as most animals did so he puffed himself up ready for them, but instead they greeted him warmly.

"Hello brother, you are new to these parts."

The ugly duckling thought they were talking to someone else and bowed his head in confusion. Then he saw his reflection in the still water.

He was no longer scruffy, grey and clumsy. He was big and white and graceful and ... just like the beautiful birds who were talking to him!

"What am I?" he said to the three swans.

"Why you're a swan, and a very handsome one too," they replied.

"A swan, a swan! I'm not an ugly duckling, I'm a swan!" he cried.

The duckling swan lived happily ever after. The three older swans became his best friends and they swam and flew everywhere together.

One day he was flying over the riverbank when he saw his mother with a new family of ducklings (every one a duck this time). He flew down and told her his story. She was delighted with his good fortune and very proud of him. From then on, whenever she saw a swan flying high above her in the sky, she would say to her ducklings, or anyone else who would listen, "That's probably my son up there."

~ THE EXCITING RANGE OF ~
JONATHAN LANGLEY TITLES
PUBLISHED BY *HARPER COLLINS:*